SEATTLE MARINERS

ALL-TIME GREATS

BY TED COLEMAN

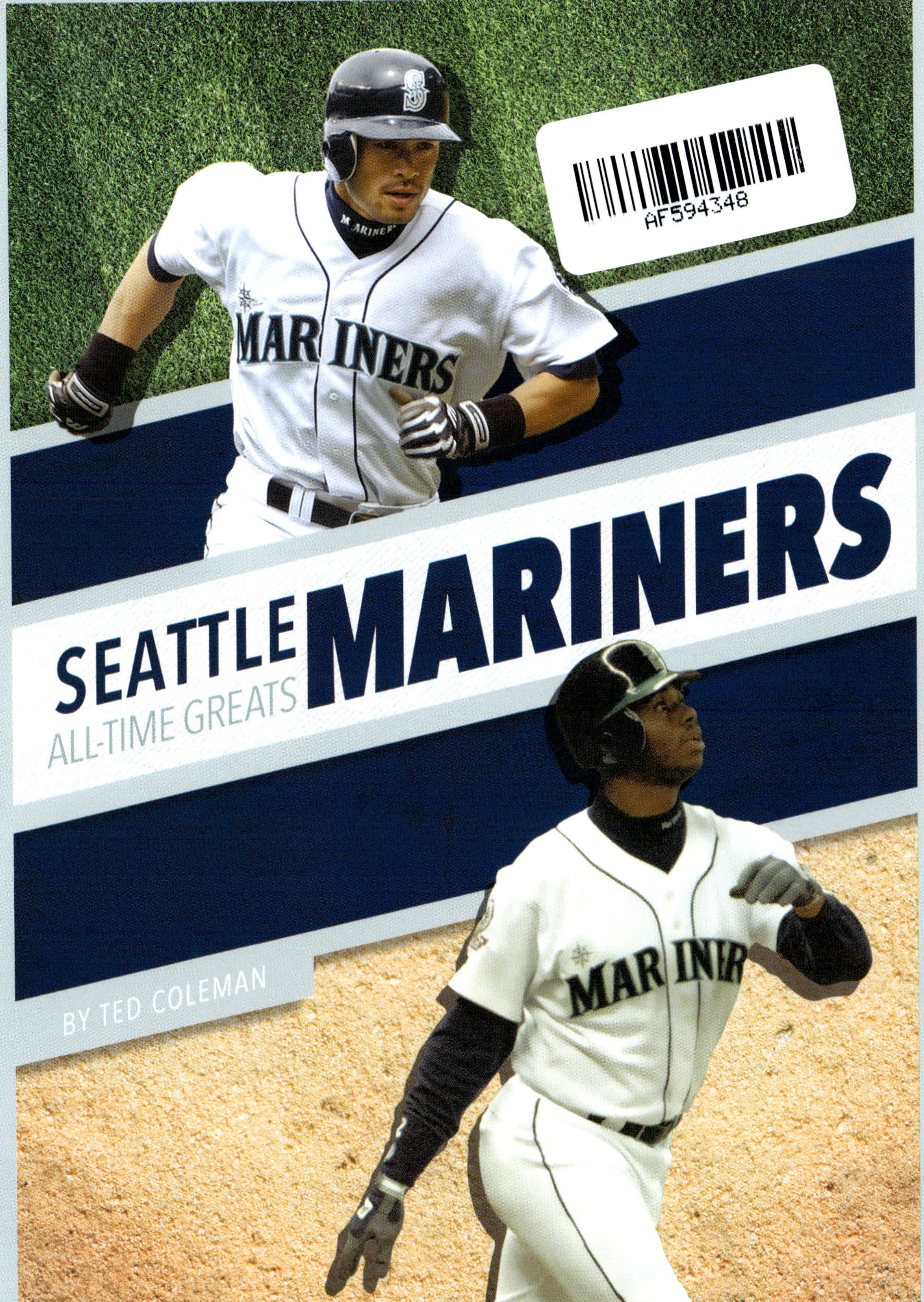

Book design by Jake Slavik
Cover design by Jake Slavik

Photographs ©: Elaine Thompson/AP Images, cover (top), 1 (top); Gary Stewart/AP Images, cover (bottom), 1 (bottom); Owen Blauman/AP Images, 4; Ray Stubblebine/AP Images, 6; John Froschauer/AP Images, 8; Al Messerschmidt/AP Images, 10; Duncan Livingston/AP Images, 12; Kevin Frayer/AP Images, 14; John Cordes/Icon Sportswire, 16; Douglas Jones/Icon Sportswire, 18; Joe Robbins/Icon Sportswire, 20

Press Box Books, an imprint of Press Room Editions.

ISBN
978-1-63494-510-3 (library bound)
978-1-63494-536-3 (paperback)
978-1-63494-586-8 (epub)
978-1-63494-562-2 (hosted ebook)

Library of Congress Control Number: 2022901760

Distributed by North Star Editions, Inc.
2297 Waters Drive
Mendota Heights, MN 55120
www.northstareditions.com

Printed in the United States of America
082022

ABOUT THE AUTHOR

Ted Coleman is a freelance sportswriter and children's book author who lives in Louisville, Kentucky, with his trusty Affenpinscher, Chloe.

TABLE OF CONTENTS

CHAPTER 1

BUILDING A WINNING TEAM 5

CHAPTER 2

REACHING THE POSTSEASON 11

CHAPTER 3

REBUILDING AND RELOADING 17

TIMELINE 22

TEAM FACTS 23

MORE INFORMATION 23

GLOSSARY 24

INDEX 24

DAVIS
21

CHAPTER 1

BUILDING A WINNING TEAM

Seattle got its first Major League Baseball (MLB) team in 1969. But it wasn't the Mariners. The team was called the Seattle Pilots. The Pilots spent only one season in Seattle. In 1970, they moved to Milwaukee and changed their name to the Brewers. But a few years later, Seattle got a new team. The Mariners began playing in 1977.

Like many new teams, the Mariners struggled at first. The team was short on stars. Even so, first baseman **Alvin Davis** became a fan favorite in the Mariners' early years. Davis had a big smile and big power. He won the

Rookie of the Year Award in 1984. Davis was the first star that Mariners fans could call their own.

Starting pitcher **Mark Langston** was another star rookie. Langston won the Rookie

Pitcher of the Year Award in 1984. He also led the American League (AL) in strikeouts that season. He went on to do it twice more. Langston also earned a trip to the All-Star Game in 1987.

Second baseman **Harold Reynolds** joined Langston on the 1987 All-Star team. Reynolds was known for his speed. In 1987, he led the AL with 60 stolen bases. Reynolds was also an excellent defender. He won three Gold Glove Awards in a row from 1988 to 1990. After he retired, Reynolds became a baseball analyst on TV.

DIEGO SEGUI

Diego Segui was a star pitcher for the Seattle Pilots in 1969. Eight years later, he returned to Seattle as a member of the Mariners. By that time, Segui was 39 years old. He was near the end of his major league career. Even so, he earned the chance to start in the Mariners' first game in Seattle. Segui is the only person to play for both of Seattle's MLB teams.

MARTINEZ
11

The Mariners were slowly building a good team. A pair of new sluggers helped speed up that process. **Edgar Martinez** was called up to the majors in 1987. He didn't see much action during his first few years. But he ended up making the All-Star team seven times during his 18-year career.

In 1988, the Mariners traded for a young outfielder named **Jay Buhner**. He had spent a couple years with the New York Yankees, but he never got much of a chance to play. That changed in Seattle. Buhner and Martinez became key parts of the first Mariners team to reach the postseason.

STAT SPOTLIGHT

CAREER GAMES PLAYED

MARINERS TEAM RECORD

Edgar Martinez: 2,055

GRIFFEY
24

CHAPTER 2

REACHING THE POSTSEASON

Center fielder **Ken Griffey Jr.** joined the Mariners in 1989. He instantly became one of the most exciting players in baseball. Griffey had great speed, and he used it to track down balls in the outfield. He also had a sweet swing with incredible power. In fact, Griffey led the league in home runs four times. And from 1990 to 1999, he made 10 straight All-Star Games.

STAT SPOTLIGHT

CAREER HOME RUNS

MARINERS TEAM RECORD

Ken Griffey Jr.: 417

One of Griffey's best seasons came in 1997. That year, he cranked out 56 home runs and won the AL Most Valuable Player (MVP) Award.

Starting pitcher **Randy Johnson** came to Seattle in 1989. The next season, he threw the first no-hitter in team history. The 6-foot-10 lefty was an intimidating presence on the mound. He had some control problems early in his career. But he fixed those problems in Seattle. Johnson became one of the best strikeout pitchers in all of baseball.

Everything came together for the Mariners in 1995. Seattle made the postseason for the first time. And Martinez provided one of the most exciting moments in team history. His two-run double against the New York Yankees helped Seattle win the AL Division Series. Fans simply refer to the play as "The Double."

FATHER AND SON

In 1990, the Mariners signed Ken Griffey Sr. The 40-year-old outfielder joined a team that included his 20-year-old son Ken Griffey Jr. The elder Griffey was at the end of a long career. But playing alongside his son was the highlight. The Griffeys became the first father and son to play together in an MLB game.

The Mariners were primed for several more postseason appearances. Shortstop **Alex Rodriguez** had played a bit in 1994 and 1995. But he burst out in 1996. He won the

AL batting title that season. He also led the league in runs and doubles. Rodriguez could hit for both average and power.

Starting pitcher **Jamie Moyer** helped Seattle's pitching depth. Moyer didn't throw very fast. But the lefty had great control. He also confused batters with a great mix of pitches. When Moyer left the Mariners in 2006, he had the most wins in team history.

Catcher **Dan Wilson** played a key role in helping Seattle's pitching staff. Wilson was one of the best defensive catchers ever. To this day, he holds many of the team's catching records.

Raul Ibanez joined Ken Griffey Jr. in the outfield. Ibanez never made the All-Star team as a Mariner. But he was a steady, reliable player. Ibanez racked up 1,077 hits during his 11 years with Seattle.

GARCIA
34
SEATTLE

CHAPTER 3

REBUILDING AND RELOADING

Johnson was traded in 1998. Griffey left after the 1999 season. And Rodriguez departed after the 2000 season. Fortunately, the Mariners still had Martinez. By then, he was near the end of a Hall of Fame career.

Freddy Garcia helped make up for the loss of Johnson. The powerful righty was one of the best pitchers in baseball in 2001. He led the AL in innings pitched and earned run average (ERA).

Second baseman **Bret Boone** helped make up for the loss of Rodriguez. Boone had been with the Mariners in the early 1990s.

When he returned in 2001, he led the AL in runs batted in (RBI).

Ichiro Suzuki was a 27-year-old rookie in 2001. But the talented outfielder had been a pro in his native Japan for years. With the Mariners, Ichiro proved that he was an elite hitter. He won the Rookie of the Year Award in 2001. That same season, he was the league's MVP. Ichiro led Seattle to an incredible 116 wins in 2001. Unfortunately for Mariners fans, the team didn't make it to the World Series.

The next generation of Mariners was led by pitcher **Felix Hernandez**. "King Felix" spent his entire 14-year career in Seattle. Hernandez made the All-Star team six times. One of his best seasons came in 2010. That year, he won the AL Cy Young Award. He also threw the team's first perfect game in 2012.

STAT SPOTLIGHT

CAREER STRIKEOUTS

MARINERS TEAM RECORD

Felix Hernandez: 2,524

Second baseman **Robinson Cano** joined the Mariners in 2014. Cano was 31 years old by that point. But in 2016, he had one of the best seasons of his career. Cano recorded 39 home runs and 103 RBI.

The Mariners weren't a great team in the 2010s. Even so, **Kyle Seager** was a steady presence at third base. Seager rarely missed a game. He also slugged 20 or more home runs in eight straight seasons.

Mitch Haniger emerged as a star in the late 2010s. The right fielder made his first All-Star Game in 2018. And in 2021, he had 39 home runs and 100 RBI. Mariners fans hoped it wouldn't be long before Haniger led Seattle back to the postseason.

SWEET LOU

The nickname "Sweet Lou" didn't really apply to manager **Lou Piniella**. Piniella was a fiery competitor. He could often be seen arguing with umpires and kicking up dirt. But Piniella was also known for winning. He led the Mariners from 1993 to 2002. Piniella has the most wins in Mariners history. And as of 2021, he was the only manager to lead the team to the postseason.

TIMELINE

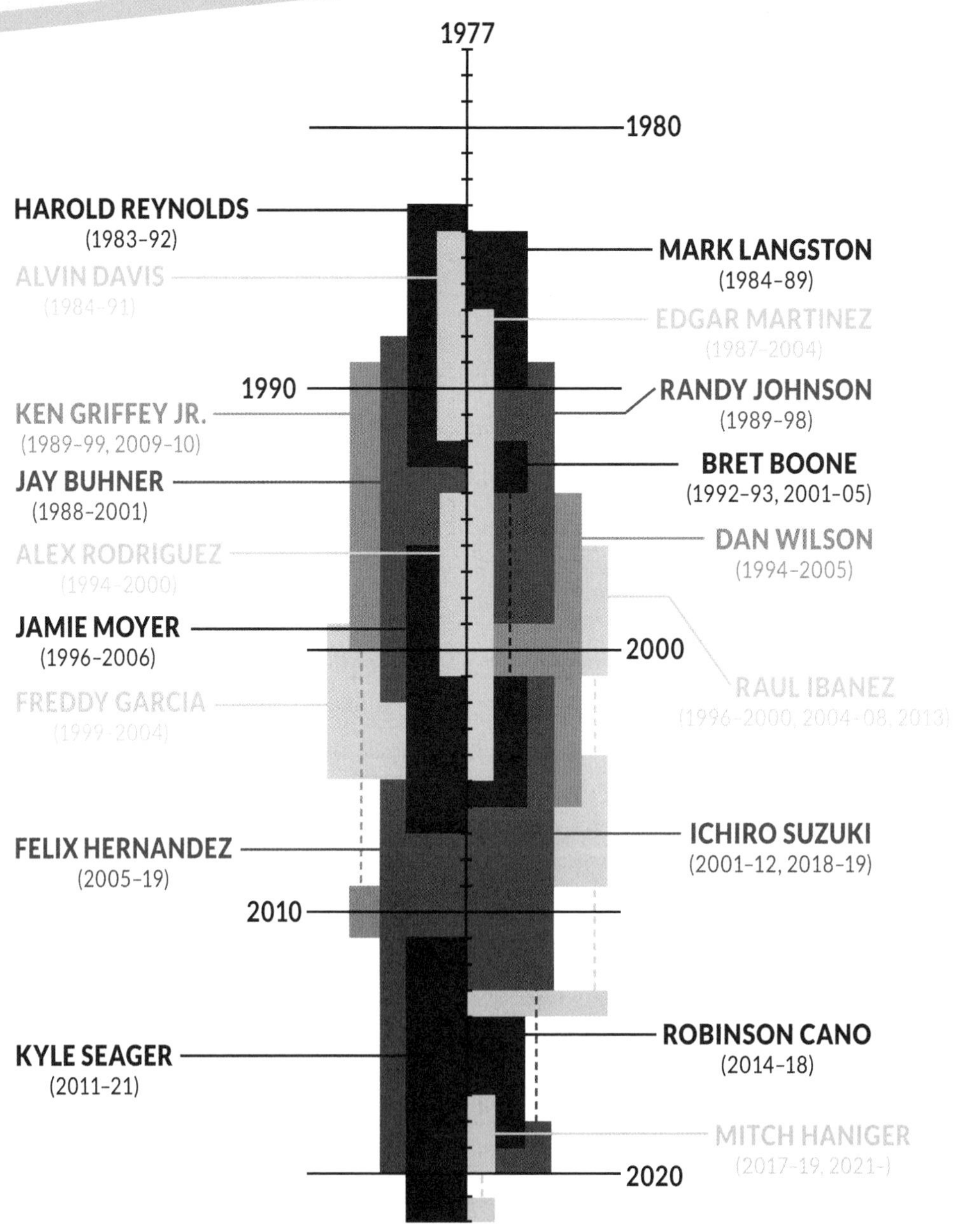

1977
1980
HAROLD REYNOLDS
(1983–92)
MARK LANGSTON
(1984–89)
ALVIN DAVIS
(1984–91)
EDGAR MARTINEZ
(1987–2004)
1990
RANDY JOHNSON
(1989–98)
KEN GRIFFEY JR.
(1989–99, 2009–10)
BRET BOONE
(1992–93, 2001–05)
JAY BUHNER
(1988–2001)
DAN WILSON
(1994–2005)
ALEX RODRIGUEZ
(1994–2000)
JAMIE MOYER
(1996–2006)
2000
RAUL IBANEZ
(1996–2000, 2004–08, 2013)
FREDDY GARCIA
(1999–2004)
ICHIRO SUZUKI
(2001–12, 2018–19)
FELIX HERNANDEZ
(2005–19)
2010
ROBINSON CANO
(2014–18)
KYLE SEAGER
(2011–21)
MITCH HANIGER
(2017–19, 2021–)
2020

TEAM FACTS

SEATTLE MARINERS

Founded: 1977

World Series titles: 0*

Key managers:

Lou Piniella (1993–2002)

840–711 (.542)

Scott Servais (2016–)

438–432 (.503)

MORE INFORMATION

To learn more about the Seattle Mariners, go to **pressboxbooks.com/AllAccess**.

These links are routinely monitored and updated to provide the most current information available.

through 2021

GLOSSARY

analyst
A person who explains the details of a game on TV.

earned run average
A measure of how many runs a pitcher gives up per nine innings.

elite
One of the best.

no-hitter
A game in which a pitcher doesn't allow any hits.

perfect game
A game in which a pitcher doesn't allow any batters to reach base.

postseason
A set of games to decide a league's champion.

rookie
A professional athlete in his or her first year of competition.

INDEX

Boone, Bret, 17–18
Buhner, Jay, 9

Cano, Robinson, 20–21

Davis, Alvin, 5–6

Garcia, Freddy, 17
Griffey, Ken Jr., 11–13, 15, 17
Griffey, Ken Sr., 13

Haniger, Mitch, 21
Hernandez, Felix, 19

Ibanez, Raul, 15

Johnson, Randy, 12–13, 17

Langston, Mark, 6–7

Martinez, Edgar, 9, 13, 17
Moyer, Jamie, 15

Piniella, Lou, 21

Reynolds, Harold, 7
Rodriguez, Alex, 14–15, 17

Seager, Kyle, 21
Segui, Diego, 7
Suzuki, Ichiro, 18–19

Wilson, Dan, 15